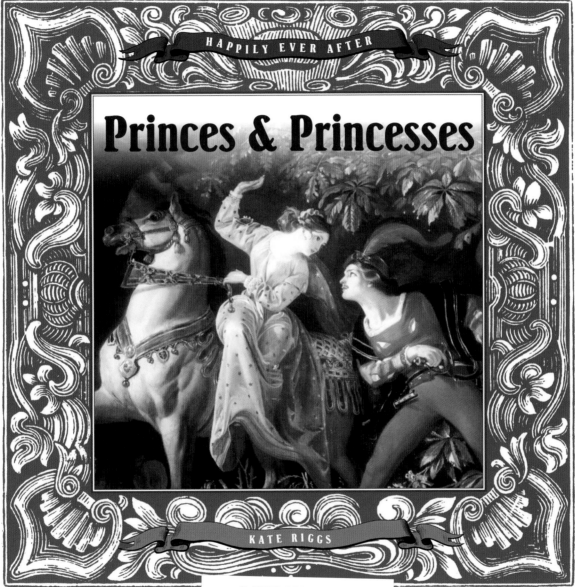

HAPPILY EVER AFTER

Princes & Princesses

KATE RIGGS

CREATIVE 🍎 EDUCATION

![COPYRIGHT]

Published by Creative Education
P.O. Box 227, Mankato, Minnesota 56002
Creative Education is an imprint of
The Creative Company
www.thecreativecompany.us

Design by Stephanie Blumenthal
Production by Christine Vanderbeek
Art direction by Rita Marshall
Printed in the United States of America

Photographs by Alamy (AF archive, Moviestore Collection Ltd), Dover Publications Inc. (120 Great Fairy Paintings; Children's Book Illustrations; Historic Costume; Imps, Elves, Fairies & Goblins), Getty Images (Henry Meynell Rheam), Graphic Frames (Agile Rabbit Editions), Mary Evans Picture Library (ARTHUR RACKHAM, Mary Evans Picture Library, Peter & Dawn Cope Collection), Shutterstock (Denis Barbulat, Roberto castillo)

Library of Congress Cataloging-in-Publication Data
Riggs, Kate.
Princes & princesses / by Kate Riggs.
p. cm. — (Happily ever after)
Summary: A primer of the familiar fairy-tale characters of princes and princesses, from what they are like to whom they interact with, plus famous stories and movies in which they have appeared.
Includes index.
ISBN 978-1-60818-243-5
1. Fairy tales. 2. Princes. 3. Princesses. I. Title.

GR550.R455 2013
398.2—dc23   2012000802

First edition
9 8 7 6 5 4 3 2 1

TABLE OF CONTENTS

*"Once upon a time,
there was a beautiful princess.
She fell in love with a handsome prince."*

Princes and princesses are people you can find in fairy tales. A fairy tale is a story about magical people and places.

Fairy tale princesses are daughters
of a king. A girl can marry a prince
to become a princess, too. In most
fairy tales, a princess is kind and
loving. She is also beautiful.

Fairy tale princes are sons of a king. They look for princesses to marry. A prince is usually brave and handsome. He likes going on adventures. He often helps a princess get out of trouble.

The prince and princess are usually the main characters in a fairy tale. Some characters try to hurt the princess or prince. Other characters are helpful.

Wicked stepmothers can be **jealous** of the princess. They might even try to kill her! Sometimes the wicked stepmother is a witch. She uses magic to cast a spell on the princess.

Fairy godmothers help princesses and princes. They use magic to give the princess or prince what they need. Other magical creatures might help, too.

In the story *Cinderella,* a girl has a
wicked stepmother who makes her do
work. One day, the prince holds a
ball at the palace. Cinderella's
fairy godmother helps her get
there. Cinderella dances with the
prince, and they fall in love.

The Disney movie *Sleeping Beauty* is about the beautiful Princess Aurora. A bad fairy casts a spell on Aurora when she is a baby. When she grows up, she **pricks** her finger and falls asleep for 100 years. A prince wakes her up with a kiss.

A princess might get into a lot of trouble. But she always gets her prince in the end.

"The prince woke the princess from the evil spell. And they lived happily ever after."

WRITE YOUR OWN FAIRY TALE

Copy this short story onto a sheet of paper.
Then fill in the blanks with your own words!

Once upon a time, there was a princess named _____.

She lived in a castle called _____. She wished that she could

_____. One day, she saw a _____. The princess felt _____.

The _____ helped the princess _____. The princess

danced with a handsome prince. His name was _____.

They lived happily ever after.

GLOSSARY

jealous—wanting what someone else has; wanting to be like someone else

pricks—cuts or pokes skin so that it bleeds

wicked—bad or evil

READ MORE

Davidson, Susanna. *The Usborne Princess Handbook*. London: Usborne, 2009.

Disney Enterprises. *Disney Princess Collection*. New York: Disney Press, 2009.

WEB SITES

Disney Princess Games
http://disney.go.com/princess/#/games/
Play games and do activities with your favorite Disney princesses.

Sleeping Beauty Coloring Pages
http://www.thedollpalace.com/coloring-pages/sec123-Sleeping-Beauty.html
Print out pages to color of Sleeping Beauty.

INDEX